My Father
Is Far Away

by Robin Ballard

Greenwillow Books   New York

Pen and ink and watercolors were used for the full-color art. The text type is
ITC Cheltenham Light. Copyright © 1992 by Robin Ballard. All rights reserved.
No part of this book may be reproduced or utilized in any form or by any means,
electronic or mechanical, including photocopying, recording, or by any
information storage and retrieval system, without permission in writing from the
Publisher, Greenwillow Books, a division of William Morrow & Company, Inc.,
1350 Avenue of the Americas, New York, NY 10019.
Printed in Hong Kong by South China Printing Company (1988) Ltd.
First Edition   10 9 8 7 6 5 4 3 2 1

Library of Congress Cataloging-in-Publication Data
Ballard, Robin.
My father is far away / by Robin Ballard.
p.   cm.
Summary: While involved in various daily activities,
a child imagines the actions of a much-missed father.
ISBN 0-688-10953-5 (trade). ISBN 0-688-10954-3 (lib.)
[1. Father and child—Fiction.   2. Loneliness—Fiction.]
I. Title. PZ7.B2125My 1992
[E]—dc20 91-29580 CIP AC

FOR C. J. B. FROM BEAN

My father is far away, doing very
important things. Maybe while I
am drawing a picture of the sun…

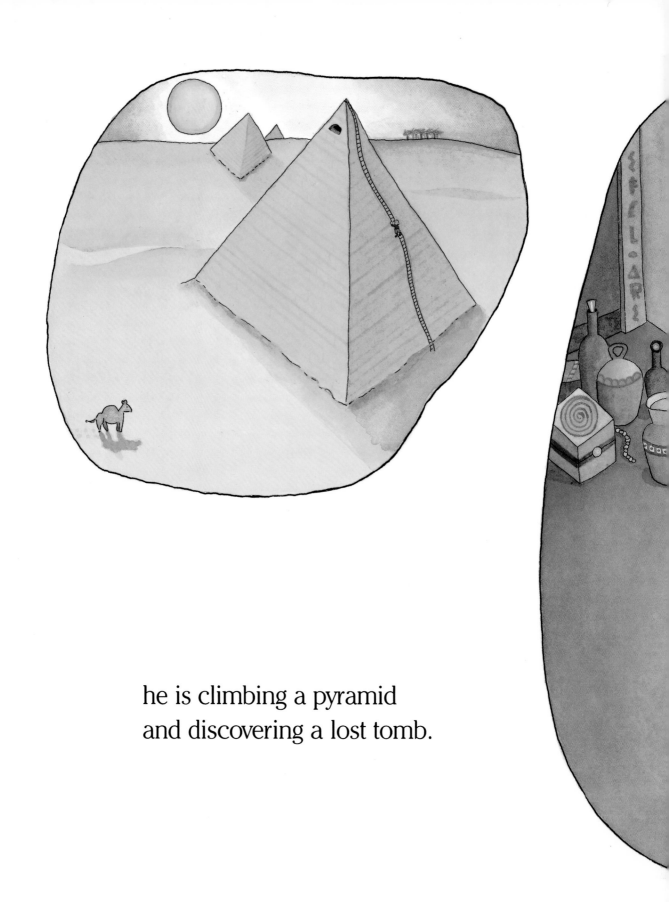

he is climbing a pyramid
and discovering a lost tomb.

In the treasure he finds
a silver ring for me.

Perhaps it is
a magic ring,
or a ring with
a curse on it.

Or maybe as I play in my room...

my father is riding a fierce black horse.

The trumpet sounds.

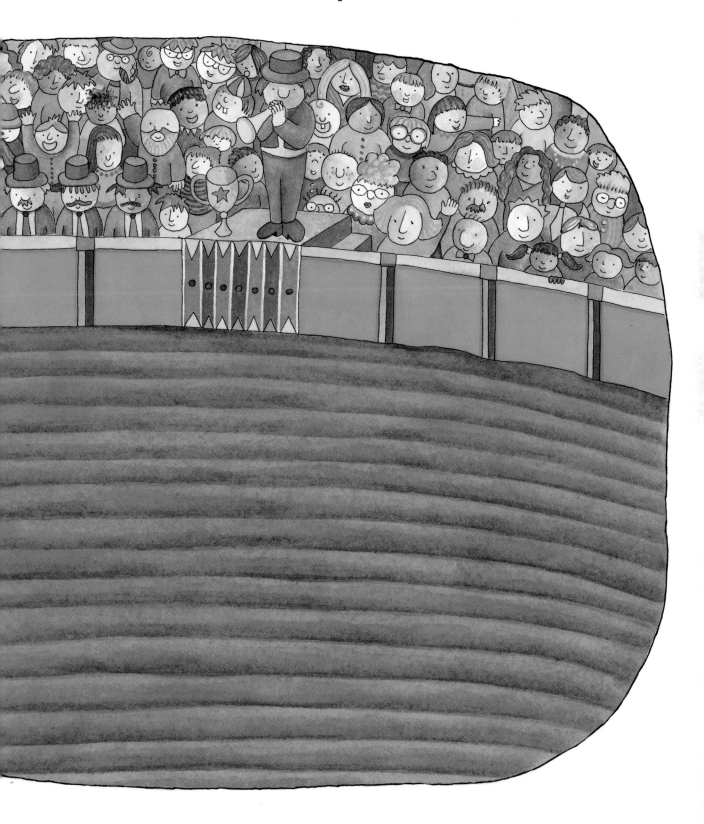

The race begins! The whole crowd cheers,
but no one cheers as loudly as I do,
watching it on TV.

And just think—as I pet
my dog on the head…

my father might be stalking
a pack of wild wolves.

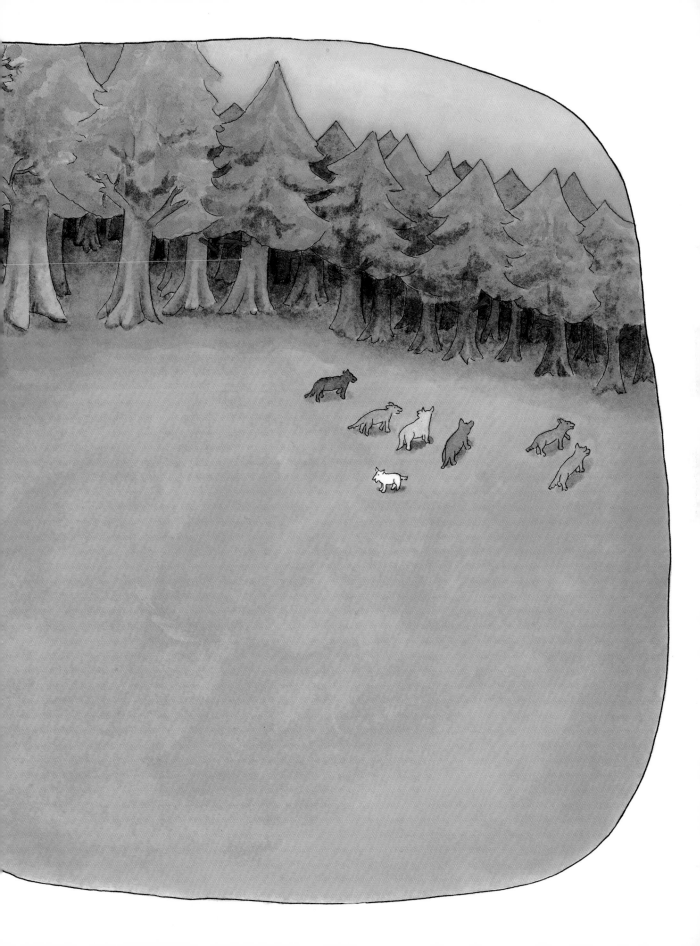

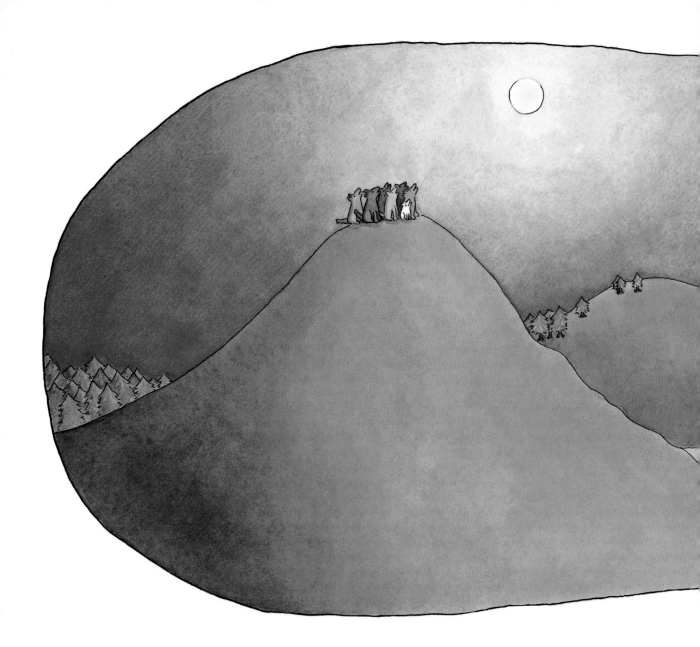

When they howl at the moon,
he just howls back.
"Who is this strange man?"
the wolves all think.

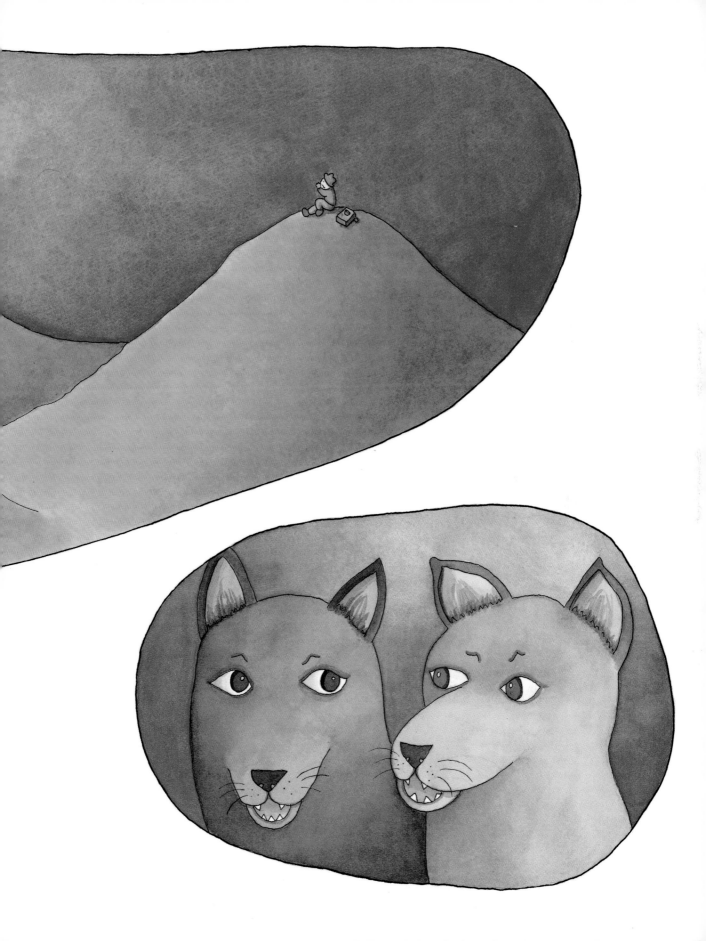

Perhaps as I take my bath…

my father is sailing on the open seas,

through nasty storms

and giant jumping fish.

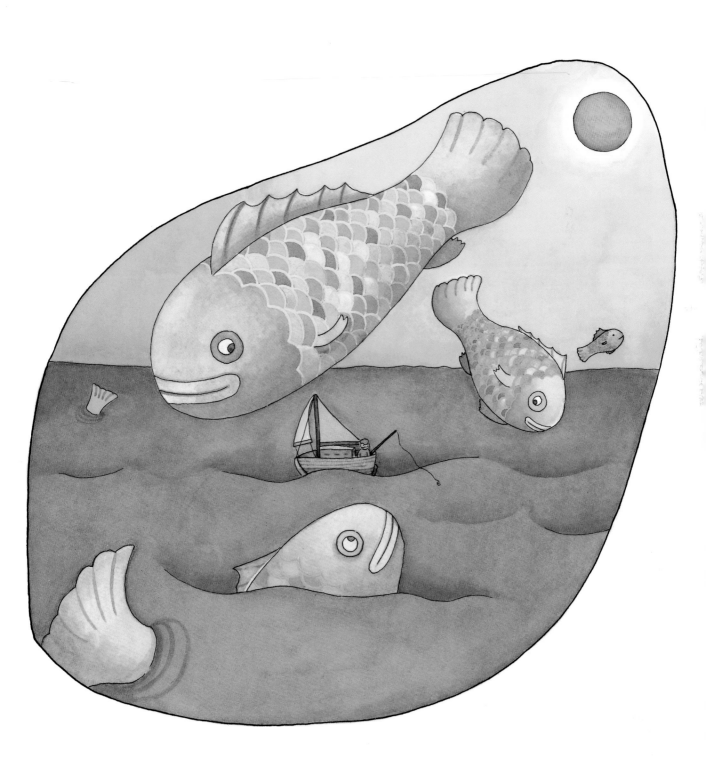

He is faster than the pirates

and finds his way
by the stars.

As I lie here in
my bed, I think
perhaps my father
is on his way
back to me.

I know he misses me, too.